THIS
TREASURY
belongs to:

A Treasury of STORIES & RHYMES

This is a Siena Book
Siena is an imprint of Parragon

Parragon
Queen Street House, 4 Queen Street, Bath, BA1 1HE

Produced by
The Templar Company plc,
Pippbrook Mill, London Road, Dorking,
Surrey RH4 1JE

Printed and bound in Singapore
ISBN 0 75252 993 5

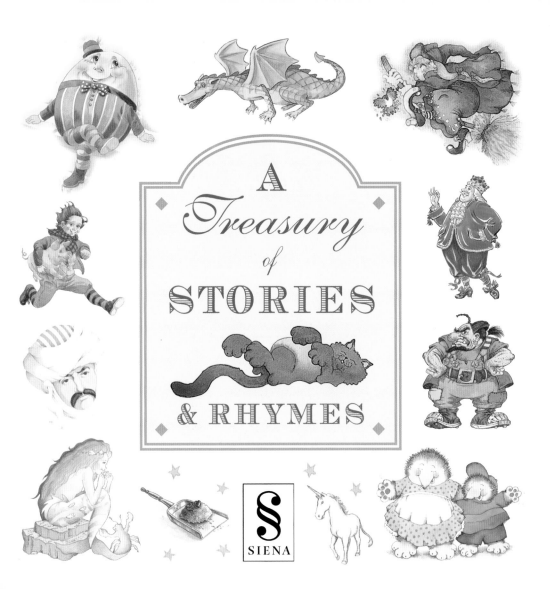

A Treasury of STORIES & RHYMES

SIENA

Contents

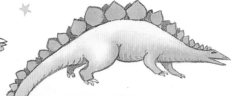

Hey! Diddle, Diddle

Hey! diddle, diddle,
The cat and the fiddle,
The cow jumped over the moon;
The little dog laughed
To see such fun,
And the dish ran away with the spoon!

Humpty, Dumpty

Humpty Dumpty sat on a wall;
Humpty Dumpty had a great fall;
All the King's horses,
And all the King's men
Couldn't put Humpty together again.

CINDERELLA

Once upon a time there was a girl called Cinderella. She lived with her kind father, her wicked stepmother, and her two mean and ugly stepsisters.

Her stepmother made Cinderella do all the housework, and wait on her and her lazy daughters hand and foot.

Cinderella had to sleep on a straw bed in the attic, while her stepsisters had beautiful rooms, with soft beds and satin sheets. Cinderella worked hard every day and did not complain to her father in case she upset him.

Her stepsisters called her Cinderella, because at night she would sit dreaming by the warm cinders of the kitchen fire. But even though she dressed in rags she was a hundred times prettier than her bad-tempered sisters in their lovely gowns.

One day an invitation from the Prince arrived from the Palace. He was holding a Grand Ball. The ugly sisters were delighted and spent days trying on dresses and planning what to wear to catch the Prince's eye. On the day of the Ball, Cinderella ran backwards and forwards between them, helping them to get ready. All the time they teased her because she was not allowed to go too.

"Ho, ho!" they chuckled. "How everyone would admire your lovely tattered dress! What a shame you cannot come with us!" And so they continued until at last they were ready, and they flounced away to the Ball. Cinderella sadly watched them go, then put her head in her hands and cried. "I wish that I could go to the Ball too," she sobbed. Little did she know that her fairy godmother was listening.

"I have come to grant your wish," said the fairy, appearing before her. "Fetch a large pumpkin from the garden." Surprised, Cinderella did as she was told and when her godmother tapped the pumpkin with her magic wand it turned into a golden coach!

Next she turned six grey mice into six fine white horses, a fat rat into a jolly coachman, and six lizards into footmen. Cinderella could hardly believe her eyes! With a last wave of her wand, the fairy godmother turned Cinderella's tatters into a lovely silver dress, with sparkling glass slippers on her feet. Cinderella was delighted! But as she climbed into the coach, her godmother warned that she must leave before midnight or everything would change back to what it had been before. With a smile and a wave, Cinderella promised not to forget.

When she arrived the Prince ran to welcome her, for she was certainly the most beautiful girl at the Ball, and as he led her into the ballroom everyone stopped to stare at her in admiration. As she passed her ugly sisters she held her breath, but they were so amazed by her beauty that they did not recognise her. The Prince could not take his eyes off Cinderella. He held her tightly in his arms and they danced all evening.

She felt so happy that she forgot all about the time. Suddenly the clock started to strike midnight! Cinderella fled from the room and out of the Palace. As she ran down the steps towards her coach one pretty glass slipper fell from her foot. Just as she reached it, the fine coach disappeared, and in its place stood the pumpkin. Pulling her tattered old cloak around her, Cinderella slipped away into the night.

Later her stepsisters came home and told her all about the mysterious beauty the Prince had danced with all evening. The only clue to her identity was a glass slipper she had left behind.

Next day the Prince issued a Royal Proclamation. He would search the land until he found the girl whose foot fitted the slipper and then he would make her his bride. The Court footmen visited every house in the country, but no one had a foot dainty enough to fit the slipper. Finally they arrived at Cinderella's home. The ugly sisters puffed and panted as they tried in vain to make the little slipper fit. Then it was Cinderella's turn. The ugly sisters gasped as it slipped onto her foot. It was a perfect fit!

Just then Cinderella's fairy godmother appeared and in a flash she was once again dressed in her finery. Much to her sister's dismay, the Prince married Cinderella the very next day and, as with all good fairy tales, they lived happily ever after.

Rock-a-Bye, Baby

Rock-a-bye, baby, on the tree top;
When the wind blows, the cradle will rock;
When the bough breaks, the cradle will fall;
Down will come baby, cradle and all.

Three Blind Mice!

Three blind mice, three blind mice,
See how they run, see how they run!
They all ran after the farmer's wife,
Who cut off their tails with a carving knife,
Did you ever see such a thing in your life,
As three blind mice?!

THE LOST GIANT

The air wobbled a bit, shimmered, swirled and with a 'whoomph' a rather bewildered, twelve-foot giant appeared. He was only a very young giant, and looked like any other young boy—except he was much larger, of course!

"Oh dear," said the giant, stepping on a bush and flattening it. Turning round he bumped into a tree, which bent over at an alarming angle.

"Stand still!" called a tiny voice.

"What was that?!" said the giant, startled. He whirled round looking for the voice and knocked the tree right over. "Where am I?"

"You're in our farmyard," yelled the small voice. "I think you're all my fault!"

"Where are you?" asked the giant.

"Down here, by the well. Bend down, carefully, and you'll see me."

And so, carefully, the giant bent down and peered at the well. Standing next to it was a little boy with blond hair and very dirty knees.

"Oh," said the giant. "You're a little boy ... aren't you afraid of me? All the little boys in my story books are afraid of giants."

"Not me," said the little boy. "I was wishing for someone to play with on my magic marble, when the air went wobbly, and I dropped it. I was crawling around in the mud looking for it when you appeared. My name's Oliver. I think I magicked you here!"

"I'm Bertie," said the giant. "I was wishing for a friend on my magic marble too!" and he fished a marble as big as a doughnut out of his pocket.

"Wow," said the little boy. "That's wonderful. I wish I could find mine."

Just then a voice called from inside the farmhouse, "Oliver, it's lunchtime!"
"Oh no," said Oliver, "that's my mum. You'd better hide in the barn."
They headed across the cornfield to the barn, and Bertie crawled inside.
"I have to go and have my lunch," Oliver explained to Bertie. "Are you hungry?"
Bertie nodded, and his tummy rumbled. It sounded just like thunder.

"I'll try and get you something to eat," Oliver promised.

Oliver gobbled his lunch up then rushed back to the barn to see his new friend. He had brought Bertie a jam sandwich, which he'd hidden in his pocket. Bertie ate it in one bite. He was too polite to tell Oliver that giants make their sandwiches as big as double beds.

"Now," said Oliver, "we have to find my marble and a way to get you back home. You're too big to stay here and Dad said he had some work to do later in the barn — so we'd better hurry."
Bertie and Oliver crept out of the barn and back to the well. They both got down on their hands and knees and started searching for the marble, but they couldn't find it. Then Bertie said he was thirsty, and peered into the well.
"It's been filled in," said Oliver.
"Good thing," said Bertie, reaching into the well, and pulling out — Oliver's marble!
"Hooray! You've found it!" cried Oliver. "Back to the barn. It's time for some magic!"

Back in the barn they rubbed their marbles and tried all the magic words they could think of, but nothing worked. Then Bertie had an idea. "The air went 'whoomph' when I arrived, didn't it? So if we make the noise backwards it might magic me home."

They said goodbye, and decided to swap marbles – like best friends do. "We might even find a way to visit each other." said Oliver.

In the distance Oliver could hear a tractor. "Oh no," he said. "Dad's coming!"

Then they rubbed their marbles hard, and said 'Phmoohw.' The air wobbled and shimmered a bit and in a flash Bertie was gone.

Outside the tractor stopped and Oliver's dad came into the barn. "That's a pretty amazing marble," he said, nodding at Oliver's hand.

"It's a giant-size one," said Oliver, and smiled secretly to himself.

Tom, Tom, The Piper's Son

Tom, Tom, the piper's son,
Stole a pig and away he run!
The pig was eat, and Tom was beat,
And Tom went roaring down the street.

Georgie Porgie

Georgie Porgie, pudding and pie,
Kissed the girls and made them cry;
When the boys came out to play,
Georgie Porgie ran away.

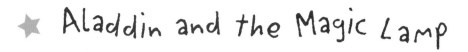

Aladdin and the Magic Lamp

Once upon a time a poor tailor died, leaving his wife and
an only son, Aladdin. One day, a stranger came to town
claiming to be Aladdin's long-lost uncle, but he was
really a wicked magician. Over supper, Aladdin's mother
begged him to find work for her son and he gladly
agreed, saying, "Tomorrow he can work for me!"
The next day the magician took Aladdin for a long
walk outside the city.

"We are here," he said at last, and they stopped for a rest. Then he muttered a magic spell and the earth split open, revealing a stone with a brass ring in it. The magician pulled the stone back to reveal a flight of steps leading down out of sight.

"At the bottom you will find a lamp," said the magician. "Bring it to me and I will reward you well." Then he gave the boy a magic ring to protect him.

Aladdin soon found the lamp and returned to his uncle. "Hurry up and give the lamp to me!" said the magician impatiently, but there was something in his voice that made Aladdin hesitate and he refused to come out. The magician was furious, for a special magic prevented him from entering the cave himself. Yet he wanted the lamp more than anything, for he knew its magic could make him rich and powerful. Cursing, he slammed the stone slab shut and fled, leaving Aladdin trapped in the cave. Poor Aladdin sat weeping and, as he did so, he accidentally rubbed the magic ring. With a puff of smoke, a huge Genie appeared. "What is your wish?" thundered the Genie. "I am the Slave of the Ring and will obey you." Aladdin begged to be taken home and soon found himself back with his mother.

"Why would the wicked man want this old lamp?" she wondered and she gave it a rub.

With a huge flash, another great genie appeared, saying: "I am the Genie of the Lamp! I will grant your every wish!" Aladdin was delighted, as he had fallen in love with the Sultan's daughter. Perhaps the Genie could help him win her hand in marriage? He asked the Genie for a bag of fine jewels and his mother visited the Sultan with them. The Sultan was amazed, but his chief adviser, the Grand Vizir, was not pleased. He wanted the Princess to marry his own son, so he persuaded the Sultan to set a difficult task for Aladdin, to prove himself worthy. The Sultan asked for forty golden bowls filled with jewels, carried by forty fine slaves. Aladdin summoned the Genie and soon slaves with bowls of gems were marching through the palace gates. The Sultan gave Aladdin his blessing at once.

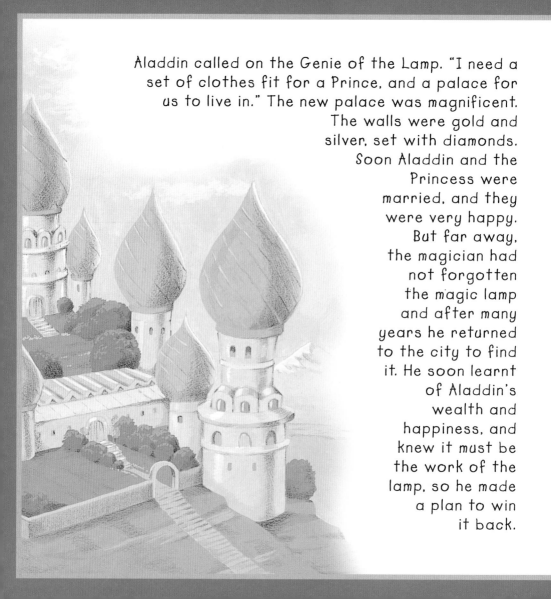

Aladdin called on the Genie of the Lamp. "I need a set of clothes fit for a Prince, and a palace for us to live in." The new palace was magnificent. The walls were gold and silver, set with diamonds. Soon Aladdin and the Princess were married, and they were very happy. But far away, the magician had not forgotten the magic lamp and after many years he returned to the city to find it. He soon learnt of Aladdin's wealth and happiness, and knew it must be the work of the lamp, so he made a plan to win it back.

The magician waited until Aladdin was away from home. Then he disguised himself as a merchant and knocked on the Palace door, offering to sell new lamps for old. The Princess was only too happy to get rid of Aladdin's old lamp, little realising its true worth. The magician snatched it and hurried away, busily plotting his revenge.

The next day the Sultan was horrified to find that the palace and his daughter had disappeared. The magician had ordered the Genie to take them to his home in Africa.

The Grand Vizier declared Aladdin must be an evil sorcerer. The angry Sultan gave Aladdin forty days to find her or he would be put to death. Aladdin was heartbroken and wept bitterly. As he did so, he rubbed his magic ring. In a flash the Genie appeared.

"Take me to the Princess," begged Aladdin and at once he was in her room and she told him all that had happened. Then Aladdin understood.
The Genie of the Lamp had a new master. Carefully he handed the Princess a small packet of powder.
"Pour this poison into the magician's wine," he said, "and all our troubles will be over."

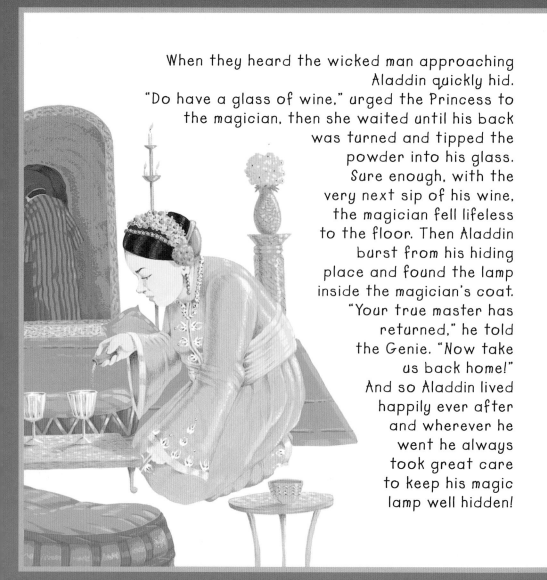

When they heard the wicked man approaching
Aladdin quickly hid.
"Do have a glass of wine," urged the Princess to
the magician, then she waited until his back
was turned and tipped the
powder into his glass.
Sure enough, with the
very next sip of his wine,
the magician fell lifeless
to the floor. Then Aladdin
burst from his hiding
place and found the lamp
inside the magician's coat.
"Your true master has
returned," he told
the Genie. "Now take
us back home!"
And so Aladdin lived
happily ever after
and wherever he
went he always
took great care
to keep his magic
lamp well hidden!

Pat-a-Cake, Pat-a-Cake

Pat-a-cake, pat-a-cake, baker's man!
Make me a cake as fast as you can:
Pat it and prick it, and mark it with B,
And put it in the oven for baby and me.

Hickory, Dickory, Dock

Hickory, Dickory, Dock,
The mouse ran up the clock;
The clock struck one;
The mouse ran down;
Hickory, Dickory, Dock.

Wobbly Witch

Wobbly Witch had a problem. She was wobbly. She wasn't wobbly when she walked down to the bottom of the garden to pick toadstools. And she wasn't wobbly when she stood over her cauldron mixing spells, or when she sat by the fire toasting rats' tails for tea. But, when she tried to fly anywhere on her broomstick — she wobbled. She wobbled and swayed and shrieked and fell to the ground in a horrible heap!

Poor Wobbly had never learned to fly a broomstick. Some witches took to it like a duck to water and never needed a single lesson. Others went to the 'Sky's The Limit School of Broomstick Flying'. But Wobbly just couldn't be bothered to learn when she was young and now she was too proud to admit that she couldn't fly. She told all her friends that she'd lost her broomstick.

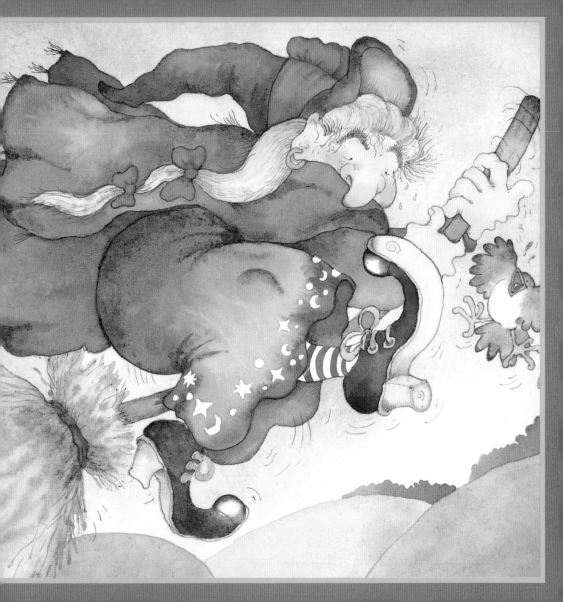

So Wobbly had to go everywhere on the bus. It was most inconvenient and very embarrassing – nasty schoolboys loved making rude remarks about her funny nose! She even had to go to the Witches' Institute on the bus. All the others flew in on smart broomsticks.

Wobbly felt quite left out as they discussed their latest models.
"Mine does 0-60 in ten seconds," said Edna.
Wobbly might never have learned to fly, if it hadn't been for the birthday present and her cat, Boris. On Wobbly's birthday the postman brought lots of birthday cards, a shiny birthday balloon, a couple of small parcels and one big one that was very long and very thin.
"What can this be, Boris?" said Wobbly to her cat, who, like all cats was very curious.

Wobbly opened the long thin parcel and her heart sank to her boots. It was a brand new, super deluxe broomstick with built-in stereo and cat seat! "To Wobbly," said the card," with love from all your friends at the Witches' Institute."

Wobbly hurriedly wrapped it up again and stuffed the broomstick under the bed.

"Stupid present," she muttered. "I hate birthdays."

That night the W.I. were meeting. Wobbly went on the bus, as usual. "I'll tell them I forgot my broomstick," she said to herself. When she arrived, there was a big surprise – her friends had laid on a lovely birthday party for her.

"Happy Birthday, Wobbly!" they shouted as she came in the door. "Where's your lovely new broomstick?"

Wobbly soon forgot to feel miserable. There was a huge birthday cake, extra wobbly jelly and delicious sandwiches. It all went well, until they started playing broomstick races. Soon, all the witches but Wobbly were whizzing up and down, cackling and having fun. "That's it!" Wobbly sulked. "I'm going home to Boris!" And she sneaked out.

But when she got home Boris was nowhere to be found. Feeling worried, Wobbly went outside and called his name. She peered into the darkness and something caught her eye. Right at the top of a tree, she saw a flash of light. It was her birthday balloon, caught on a branch.

Suddenly, the branch shook. "Miaeeeeeew!" It was Boris! He had chased the balloon to the top of the tallest tree in the garden and now he was stuck! "Oh, you silly cat!" shrieked Wobbly. "How am I going to get you down from there!"

She fetched a ladder, but it only reached halfway up the tree. There was only one thing for it — she dashed inside and fetched her new broomstick.

"Don't worry, Boris!" she cried. "I'll rescue you!"

She closed her eyes and took a deep breath...

Up she went, up into the sky without a single wobble! Poor Boris was clinging on to the tree for dear life. Wobbly grabbed him, put him on the broomstick behind her, then swept down to a smooth landing. Wobbly leapt off and hopped with glee.

"Did you see that, Boris?" she cackled. "I can fly! Come on! We have a party to go to!" Soon they were back at the party, joining in the races.

"I couldn't fly because I was afraid," she said to Boris later when they got home. "But tonight I was so worried you would fall and hurt yourself — I forgot to be afraid!" From that day on, Wobbly flew everywhere on her smart new broomstick. She's still called Wobbly, but she doesn't wobble any more!

If

If all the world were apple pie,
And all the seas were ink,
And all the trees were bread and cheese,
What should we have for drink?

Little Jack Horner

Little Jack Horner,
Sat in a corner,
Eating a Christmas pie.
He put in his thumb,
And pulled out a plum,
And said, "What a good boy am I."

RAPUNZEL

There once lived a man and his wife who were good, kind people, but they were unhappy, as they longed for a child. The woman grew so sad that she fell ill and took to her bed. From her window she could see fresh green herbs growing in the garden of the big house that stood next door, and begged her husband to fetch some to make her better.

The house belonged to a witch and the garden was surrounded by a high wall to keep everyone away. That night the man climbed the wall to take some of the herbs for his wife to eat, but the furious witch was waiting!

She agreed to let him go on one condition - that if they should have a child they would give it to her. The man was so terrified that he agreed and ran for home.

Some months later, his wife had a baby daughter and they were overjoyed. But soon after her birth the witch came and took the little baby away. The man and his wife were grief-stricken but how ever hard they searched, they could not find her. The witch raised the little girl all alone and named her Rapunzel. When Rapunzel was sixteen the witch locked her away in a tall tower in the middle of the forest and each day she would visit her and call out: "Rapunzel, Rapunzel, let down your hair!" Then Rapunzel would let down her two long plaits of golden hair from the window and the witch would climb up.

Then one day a Prince came riding through the forest and heard Rapunzel singing sweetly. He hid behind a tree when the witch arrived and watched as she clambered up into the tower. He thought Rapunzel was the most beautiful girl he had ever seen, and so when the witch had gone, he went to the tower and called: "Rapunzel, Rapunzel, let down your hair!" Then he climbed up Rapunzel's plaits and jumped inside the room. Rapunzel was astonished to see this handsome stranger, but she fell in love at once and agreed to be his bride. Soon they they had planned her escape. Each day the Prince brought her silk thread which she weaved into a ladder, and carefully hid away.

But one day she let slip about the Prince, and the witch was furious! She took out a pair of scissors and cut off Rapunzel's beautiful golden hair. Then she took Rapunzel away into a wilderness and left her there all alone. That evening the witch lay in wait for the Prince, who called out: "Rapunzel, Rapunzel, let down your hair!"

The witch tied Rapunzel's plaits to a hook on the wall and threw them out of the window. In a flash the Prince had scrambled up and leapt inside, but what a shock he got to find the horrible witch awaiting him, instead of Rapunzel! "Ha, ha, ha!" she cackled. "I have hidden Rapunzel far away and you will never see her pretty face again."

The Prince was filled with despair and leapt from the window. He landed in a rose bush and was blinded by the sharp thorns. Away he wandered into the forest, weeping for his lost love. He strayed through the wilderness for many weeks and with each step his heart grew heavier and heavier.

Then one day he heard someone singing sweetly. He had heard that song once before. Could it be Rapunzel? He stumbled blindly towards the sound and Rapunzel looked up and saw her Prince at once. She ran into his arms and held him close. As she wept for joy two of her tears dropped on his eyes and suddenly he could see once more!

"You will never be parted from me again," he promised Rapunzel, and so they made their way to his kingdom and there they were married. They heard no more from the wicked witch and Rapunzel and her Prince lived happily ever after.

Diddle, Diddle, Dumpling

Diddle, diddle, dumpling, my son John,
Went to bed with his trousers on;
One shoe off, one shoe on,
Diddle, diddle, dumpling, my son John.

Hickety Pickety

Hickety, Pickety, my black hen,
She lays eggs for gentlemen;
Sometimes nine and sometimes ten.
Hickety, Pickety, my black hen!

BARON BEEFBURGER

A very long time ago, the evil Baron Beefburger lived in a great castle. He was always grumpy and made his courtiers' lives a misery. There was nothing he liked more than hurling custard pies at people. His cooks worked day and night cooking the Baron's favourite beefburgers and an endless supply of custard pies.

In the castle lived the beautiful Princess Petunia and a knight called Sir Fightalot, who were very fond of each other. But the evil baron wanted the princess for himself, and so one day when Sir Fightalot was out riding he invited her to dinner – and threatened to put a custard pie in her bed if she didn't come!

Sir Fightalot was furious when he found out, so with the help of his friend, Friar Tuckshop, he made a plan.

The next day Sir Fightalot and Friar Tuckshop set off to find the only creature in the land more powerful than the baron – a dragon who lived in a cave far away. A few years earlier the baron had sent the entire army to kill the dragon and make him into an umbrella stand. They didn't succeed, of course, but the dragon was not too pleased with the baron, so they thought he might be happy to help. Still, Sir Fightalot's knees were knocking as they reached the dragon's cave. There was always a chance he might eat them.

But they need not have worried, because the dragon was feeling lonely. He was fed up with people either running away from him or trying to kill him, so he was pleased to see some friendly faces, and they found themselves being entertained with tea and fairy cakes. They explained about the baron's latest tricks, and together with the dragon (whose name was Humphrey) they devised a clever plan...

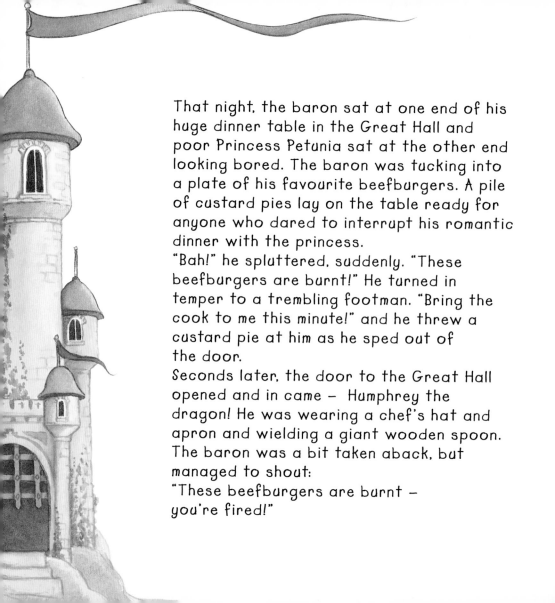

That night, the baron sat at one end of his huge dinner table in the Great Hall and poor Princess Petunia sat at the other end looking bored. The baron was tucking into a plate of his favourite beefburgers. A pile of custard pies lay on the table ready for anyone who dared to interrupt his romantic dinner with the princess.

"Bah!" he spluttered, suddenly. "These beefburgers are burnt!" He turned in temper to a trembling footman. "Bring the cook to me this minute!" and he threw a custard pie at him as he sped out of the door.

Seconds later, the door to the Great Hall opened and in came – Humphrey the dragon! He was wearing a chef's hat and apron and wielding a giant wooden spoon. The baron was a bit taken aback, but managed to shout:

"These beefburgers are burnt – you're fired!"

"No," replied Humphrey. "You're fired," and he breathed on the baron's beefburgers. In a flash they were reduced to ashes. Sir Fightalot and Friar Tuckshop appeared.

"Our friend Humphrey is going to be the new cook," said Sir Fightalot to the baron. "If you ever pester Princess Petunia again, or throw another custard pie, he'll burn your beefburgers to a cinder. Is that clear?"

The baron spluttered and sighed, but he knew that he was beaten. He couldn't argue with a big fire-breathing dragon.

After that, life was a lot easier at the castle. The baron still threw the odd custard pie, but the dragon would burn his beefburgers that night to teach him a lesson. The princess was so impressed with Sir Fightalot that she married him. Humphrey stayed on as the castle cook and was very happy. He loved cooking and, best of all, he wasn't lonely any more. And if the baron fancied a custard pie – he had to make it himself!

Little Bo Peep

Little Bo Peep has lost her sheep
And doesn't know where to find them;
Leave them alone, and they'll come home
Bringing their tails behind them.

Old Mother Hubbard

Old Mother Hubbard
Went to the cupboard
To get her poor dog a bone;
But when she came there
The cupboard was bare,
And so the poor dog had none.

The Little Mermaid

Once there was a little mermaid Princess, who lived with her father, The Mer King, and her five older sisters, in a beautiful coral palace beneath the sea. She loved her life under the sea, but she often daydreamed about visiting the world above the waves. Then, at sunset on her fifteenth birthday, she was allowed to visit the surface at last.

She watched spellbound as a fine ship came sailing by. Out on deck she could see a handsome Prince looking out to sea.
Suddenly there was a loud clap of thunder and dark storm clouds gathered. The waves rose high and the ship was tossed up and down, before finally sinking into the sea.

The little mermaid was very frightened, but she knew she must save the Prince. She found him clinging to a plank of wood, and gently carried him to shore.

As he lay upon the beach a young girl found him and called for help. The Prince opened his eyes and believed that she was the one who had saved him.

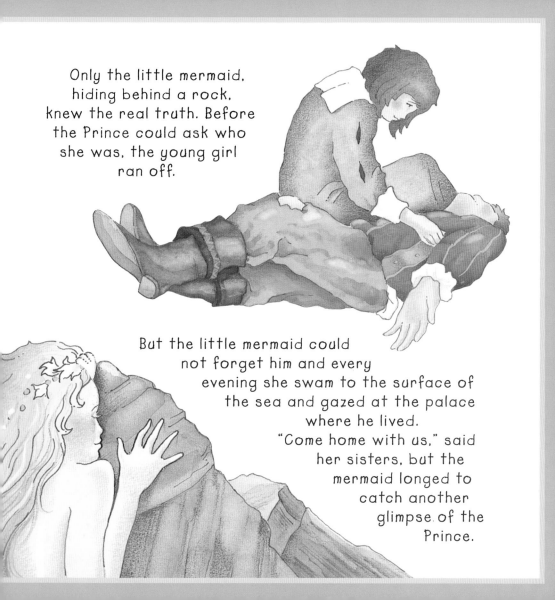

Only the little mermaid, hiding behind a rock, knew the real truth. Before the Prince could ask who she was, the young girl ran off.

But the little mermaid could not forget him and every evening she swam to the surface of the sea and gazed at the palace where he lived.

"Come home with us," said her sisters, but the mermaid longed to catch another glimpse of the Prince.

"You cannot share his life,"
her sisters told her. "You
have a silver tail and will
never be able to walk on
dry land. You must forget him."
But the mermaid could think of nothing
else. She would not be happy until she
was rid of her tail and able to join
her Prince. So she went to visit
the wicked Sea Witch to see if
she could help, and they made
a terrible deal.

In return for a potion to turn her tail into legs, the little mermaid gave the witch her lovely voice. The witch told her that every step she took would be like walking on knives, and she would never again be a mermaid or be able to return home. But the mermaid could think only of her Prince and agreed to this dreadful demand at once.

The Prince found the little mermaid lying on the steps of his palace the next day. She could not speak, but he welcomed the beautiful stranger to his home, and she soon captivated his court with her sweet smile and graceful dancing.
As the weeks passed the Prince showed nothing but kindness to the mermaid, and grew to love her as dearly as if she were his own sister. He never once thought of marrying her.
And so in time it was arranged that the Prince should marry a neighbouring Princess, and he set off on the Royal Ship to meet her. The Prince was overjoyed, for she was the same girl who had knelt by his side on the beach. "You are the one who saved me!" he cried. The heartbroken little mermaid could only watch in silence, and could not explain the truth.

And so the happy couple were married at once. That night, the sad little mermaid gazed out to sea. Having failed to win his heart, she would soon turn to foam on the sea, as the witch had told her. Just then, her sisters rose up from the waves.

"Take this knife," they called. "The Sea Witch says that if you kill the Prince and let his blood fall on your feet you will become a mermaid again!" But the little mermaid could not kill her Prince for she loved him too much. So she flung the knife far out to sea and jumped overboard. But instead of dissolving into foam, she felt herself being raised into the air by a thousand beautiful spirits and she was filled with joy.

She could see the Prince and his bride sleeping peacefully far below her and she was truly glad they had found happiness together.

Ride a Cock-Horse

Ride a cock-horse to Banbury Cross,
To see a fine lady upon a white horse,
With rings on her fingers and bells on her toes
She shall have music wherever she goes.

Yankee Doodle

Yankee Doodle came to town,
Riding on a pony,
He stuck a feather in his cap
And called it macaroni.

The Giant Pumpkins

Fortyodd was a giant. He was called Fortyodd because
he was forty-odd times as tall as a man! If you spread
your arms wide, it wouldn't be as wide as his smile.
Fortyodd was a gardener, and loved his job looking
after the Great Forest. He called it his lawn.
One morning, his friend Fiftytimes knocked on the door
of his shed, which was nine times as big as a
barn. "Come in," smiled Fortyodd. "Would you
like a vat of tea?"
"Yes please," replied Fiftytimes. "Two sugars."
Fortyodd scooped up two wheelbarrows of
sugar and stirred the tea with a lamppost.
"I've got bad news for you," said Fiftytimes.
"Old Twoscore is planning to enter his prize
cabbage in the Harvest Show next week.
He's hoping to win the Big Veg prize."
"I didn't know Twoscore had a prize
cabbage," said Fortyodd, rather uneasily.
"I passed his cabbage patch yesterday,"
said Fiftytimes. "He's got a
handsome crop."

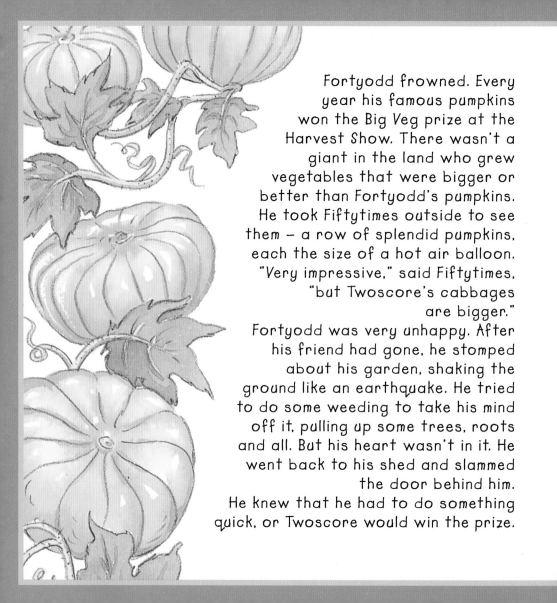

Fortyodd frowned. Every year his famous pumpkins won the Big Veg prize at the Harvest Show. There wasn't a giant in the land who grew vegetables that were bigger or better than Fortyodd's pumpkins. He took Fiftytimes outside to see them – a row of splendid pumpkins, each the size of a hot air balloon. "Very impressive," said Fiftytimes, "but Twoscore's cabbages are bigger."

Fortyodd was very unhappy. After his friend had gone, he stomped about his garden, shaking the ground like an earthquake. He tried to do some weeding to take his mind off it, pulling up some trees, roots and all. But his heart wasn't in it. He went back to his shed and slammed the door behind him.

He knew that he had to do something quick, or Twoscore would win the prize.

Fortyodd was very proud of
the row of Big Veg rosettes
over his fireplace, and couldn't
bear the thought of not having a
new one to pin up this year. He
took down the gardening book that
his grandfather, old Seventysomething,
had compiled. It was full of great tricks
and tips. Fortyodd put on his reading
glasses (two telescope lenses from an
observatory held in bent scaffolding)
and studied the book carefully. Before
long he found just the thing – a recipe
for Plant Growth Formula.
That evening, Fortyodd made up the
recipe. It took hours of mixing,
measuring and stirring. Then he went
outside to his pumpkin patch. The
pumpkins looked huge and golden in the
moonlight. Fortyodd used a fire hose to
spray the magic formula over his
pumpkins. It twinkled electric green in
the darkness. Then off he went to bed.

Next morning, Fortyodd woke at eight, and was surprised to see that it was still dark. He tried to open his door, but it wouldn't budge. So he went to the window, but all he could see was a wall of bright orange. Rather worried, Fortyodd took the door off its hinges and found that the doorway was blocked by the biggest pumpkin he had ever seen! It was acres across from side to side. Fortyodd squeezed out and climbed onto the top of the enormous vegetable. It was like standing on an orange mountain, and there were rows of other orange mountains around it. The huge pumpkins surrounded his shed, and seemed in danger of crushing it. The formula had certainly worked! Fortyodd wasn't sure what to do next, but he knew that, one way or another, it would involve a lot of pumpkin-eating!

Everyone agreed that Fortyodd's pumpkins were the biggest Big Veg they had ever seen. People flocked from miles around to see them. Families of giants had their photographs taken in front of the great pumpkin range. Passing dragons looked down at them in astonishment. Dwarf mountaineers climbed them and stuck flags in the top.

Twoscore's prize cabbages won the Big Veg rosette at the Harvest Show, of course. Everyone said it was a shame. Fortyodd's pumpkins were the biggest in the world, but even with his friend Fiftytimes' help, he couldn't budge them an inch, let alone take them to the show!

Still, he knew one thing – his grandfather would have been proud of him!

Mary, Mary, Quite Contrary

Mary, Mary, quite contrary,
How does your garden grow?
With silver bells and cockle shells
And pretty maids all in a row.

★ Ali Baba and the Forty Thieves ★

In a far away land there lived two brothers. Ali Baba was poor, but his brother Cassim was wealthy and lived in a fine house. He had a greedy wife who always wanted more. One day Ali Baba was working in the forest when he heard some men on horses approaching, and he hid in a tree in case they were robbers. He watched as they stopped by a great rock face.

"Open, Sesame!" cried their leader, and a secret door swung open. Ali Baba counted as they went inside. "Forty robbers! I wonder what they have hidden in that cave." Later the men came out and rode away. Then Ali Baba went and stood by the rock face. "Open, Sesame!" he cried. The rock door slid open and he ran inside.

The cave was full of wonderful treasures – silk and jewels and great chests of gold coins! Ali Baba was overjoyed! Now he would never be hungry again. Quickly he took as much gold as he could carry and hurried home.
His wife was delighted, but when his brother's wife found out she was jealous. Ali Baba told his brother what had happened and offered to share the treasure.

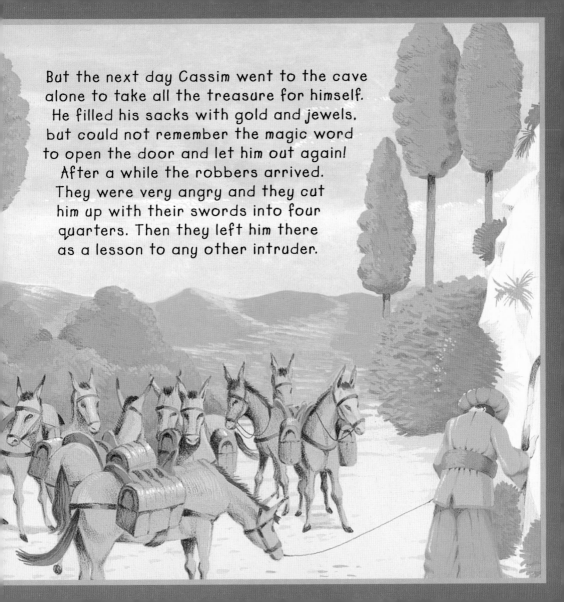

But the next day Cassim went to the cave
alone to take all the treasure for himself.
He filled his sacks with gold and jewels,
but could not remember the magic word
to open the door and let him out again!
After a while the robbers arrived.
They were very angry and they cut
him up with their swords into four
quarters. Then they left him there
as a lesson to any other intruder.

That night Ali Baba went to look for Cassim and was horrified when he found him. Sadly, he took the four quarters of his body home. But Ali Baba's clever servant, Morgiana, went to fetch a cobbler to stitch the body back together so it could be buried. She brought him to the house blindfolded, so he would not know where he was. Meanwhile, the Forty Thieves were amazed to find that the body was missing.

"Someone else knows our secret password!" cried the Captain. "He must be found!"

One of the robbers was sent to the city. In return for a gold coin, the cobbler soon led the robber to the very door, for he remembered the way he had gone, and the robber marked the door with a cross.

But when Morgiana saw the cross she guessed what had happened, and put crosses on all the other doors so that when the robbers returned they could not find the house.

The next day the Captain himself made the cobbler take him to the house. Then he went to the market, bought forty mules and forty oil jars, and returned to his cave. Each robber climbed inside a jar, and the mules carried the jars to the city.

Disguised as an oil merchant, the Captain went to Ali Baba's house and asked for a bed for the night, and kind Ali Baba agreed. The Captain left his mules in the yard outside, with the men in the jars ready to fight when the Captain gave the word.

But clever Morgiana soon discovered the men and knew they were the robbers come to attack her master. So she boiled a large pan of oil and tipped it over each of the robbers until they were all dead. Later, the Captain went to give the order to fight and found his men killed. He fled over the wall and was gone.

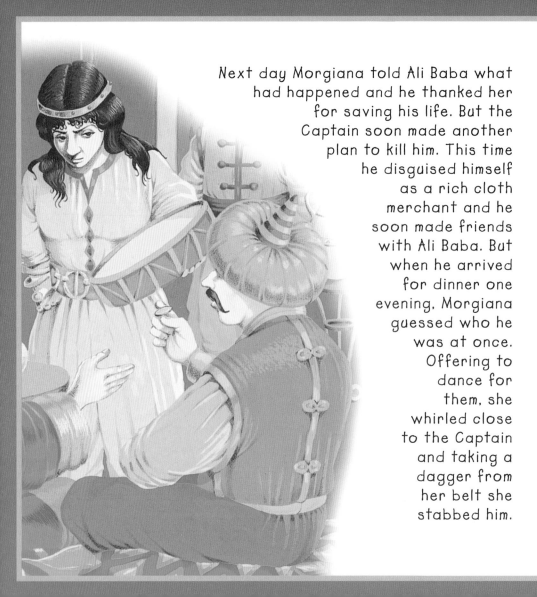

Next day Morgiana told Ali Baba what had happened and he thanked her for saving his life. But the Captain soon made another plan to kill him. This time he disguised himself as a rich cloth merchant and he soon made friends with Ali Baba. But when he arrived for dinner one evening, Morgiana guessed who he was at once. Offering to dance for them, she whirled close to the Captain and taking a dagger from her belt she stabbed him.

Ali Baba was amazed when she explained he was really the robber Captain come in disguise to kill him! Ali Baba was so grateful to her, that he gave his permission for her to marry his son, for the two had long been in love.
And so Ali Baba's family lived happily ever after and in time he told his son the secret of the cave, and the years passed in wealth and happiness for them all.

Fiddle-De-Dee

Fiddle-de-dee, Fiddle-de-dee,
The fly shall marry the bumble-bee.
They went to the church and married was she:
The fly has married the bumble-bee.

⋆ A Dog Named Brian ⋆

Wimple the Witch was having trouble with her cat. Now, as you know, all witches need a cat. No cat, no spells. "You're a big useless heap of fur," she shrieked at Montgomery, who was fast asleep, snoring. Wimple drew back her large foot and booted him across the room. Montgomery spun in mid-air and came to rest on his paws with a faint look of surprise. His feelings were more hurt than anything. True, he had slowed down lately, but he was getting on a bit now. He'd used up eight-and-a-half lives and all he wanted was some peace.

Wimple glared at Montgomery, who had gone straight back to sleep, paws in the air.

"Right!" she screamed. "That's it!" It was time to get another cat. In a flash she was on her broomstick heading to the Cat Agency.

"I want a hardworking black cat with a streak of genius. Experience in turning princes into frogs and vice versa preferred," she said, to the witch behind the counter.

"No cats. We've had a run on them. All we've got left is a dog called Brian." said the assistant, and she went and fetched a huge dog who looked rather miserable. He knew what would happen. No one ever wanted him. He'd spent three years learning to be a Witch's Personal Assistant but nobody would hire him.

"I'll take him!" said Wimple. She was a desperate witch.

The first problem was that Brian was far too big to ride on a broomstick, so Wimple had to walk home, carrying her broomstick with Brian padding along behind. Back home, she decided to try him out straight away on a spell.

"Right, Brian, sit and stare at the cauldron until it starts to bubble. I'll go and find that good-for-nothing cat and tell him he's fired!"

Brian sat and stared at the cauldron, but it was so big he couldn't see inside it. So he put his paws up on the top of the cauldron to look in and check if it was bubbling.

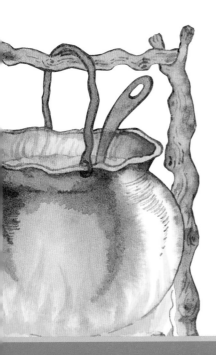

The big pot swayed
and tilted and crash! It
toppled over. All the bubbling
liquid flowed onto the floor –
and over Montgomery who was busy
escaping from Wimple.
Montgomery felt very strange for
a minute and then turned into a Brussel sprout.
"You stupid dog! Quick, we'll have to mix another spell,"
cried Wimple, and sent him out into the garden to fetch
some toadstools.

Unfortunately he trampled all over Wimple's magic herbs
in the process. Wimple was furious.
When Wimple had calmed down, she mixed the spell and
changed Montgomery back, none the worse for wear.
But then she dropped her recipe book into the cauldron
and it disappeared in a puff of smoke. That was the last
straw. Brian and Montgomery made a hasty exit. Wimple
was hopping mad. She jumped up and down until – bump!
Her head hit the shelf where she
kept her secret jars. A big jar
marked Frog Mixture toppled
over, the thick green liquid
pouring down onto
Wimple's head.

When Brian and Montgomery crept in a little later, Wimple was gone. There was just a small, green frog sitting on the floor. They saw the jar lying next to it and guessed at once what had happened.

They ran over to where Wimple's recipe book was kept, but there was no sign of it!

They would just have to try and remember the right spell. Montgomery fetched some squashed herbs. Brian took down a jar of Pickled Slugs and some All Purpose Slime. They mixed the ingredients in a pot and stirred it with their paws, then sat and stared hard. Slowly, it began to bubble. With that, the frog leapt into the pot with a plop.

And out came – Wimple! She was a little slimy, but it was definitely her.

"I was wrong about you two," she said taking out a big juicy bone for Brian and a tasty kipper for Montgomery. "A witch couldn't have two better assistants. What a team!"

Dance To Your Daddy

Dance to your daddy, My little babby;
Dance to your daddy, My little lamb.
You shall have a fishy
On a little dishy,
You shall have a fishy
When the boat comes in.

The Lion and The Unicorn

The lion and the unicorn
Were fighting for the crown;
The lion beat the unicorn
All around the town.
Some gave them white bread,
And some gave them brown;
Some gave them plum cake,
And drummed them out of town.

THE EMPEROR'S NEW CLOTHES

Many years ago, in a far off land, there lived an Emperor who had a great interest in one thing only – his clothes! He took no interest in his food, his entertainment, his soldiers, or his government. As long as he was beautifully and expensively dressed he was happy, and he would strut about showing off to anyone who cared to watch.

Strangers often visited the large, wealthy city he lived in.

One day two men arrived at the city gate. They were dishonest swindlers pretending to be weavers.

"We can weave a cloth more beautiful than you could imagine," they said. "And what is more, it's magical. Only clever people can see it. Stupid people think it's invisible!"

When the Emperor heard their claims, he was curious. "I should like a suit made from this cloth," he thought. "Then I would find out which of my ministers are clever, and which are stupid." So the Emperor gave the men a large bag full of gold coins, and told them to make him some of the magical cloth. The swindlers set up their weaving looms and pretended to start work.

After a while the Emperor was curious to see his new material, but he remembered that only clever people could see it. He decided to find out how clever the Prime Minister was, and sent him along to take a look. But the poor Prime Minister was astonished to find he could see nothing at all! "I must be stupid!" he thought. He would have to pretend he could see the cloth so no-one would find out!

So the Prime Minister told the Emperor it was the most splendid cloth he had ever seen, and the swindlers laughed to think they had fooled him. Next, the Emperor sent the Chancellor to see what he thought.

"Isn't it beautiful?" asked the weavers, holding up a pretend length of cloth.

"L...lovely," stammered the Chancellor, who could see nothing at all. And he went back and told the Emperor that the cloth was superb. The Emperor could wait no longer. He went to see for himself, followed by his courtiers.

"See your Majesty!" cried the Prime Minister and the Chancellor. "Such texture! Such glorious colour!" The Emperor was amazed for he could see nothing at all. "This is terrible," he thought. "Am I stupid? Am I not fit to be Emperor?" He decided at once to pretend. "It has my complete approval," he announced. "It is delightful."

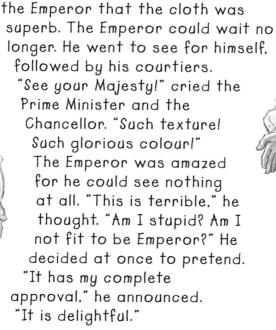

His puzzled courtiers gathered round and stared. They, too, saw nothing, but no one wanted to appear stupid. "Exquisite!" they cried.

And so the Emperor ordered a new suit made from the cloth, to wear at the grand procession the next day. He arrived early in the morning, eager to try on the suit.

"It is so soft, your Majesty," said the swindlers, "that it will feel as if you are wearing nothing at all!"

The Emperor took off all his clothes, and the swindlers pretended to dress him. He gazed at the mirror, admiring his fine new suit. "What a perfect fit!" exclaimed his courtiers. "It's a wonderful suit!"

"Splendid!" said the Emperor. And all the time he was really wearing nothing at all!

At last it was time for the procession to begin. The Emperor walked along proudly leading the way, and all the people stared. To their amazement they could see that he was not wearing a stitch of clothing! But no one dared to admit it for fear of being thought stupid. Meanwhile the swindlers packed up, grabbed their bags of gold and fled the city!

Then one little boy piped up, "But the Emperor has nothing on!"

Everyone gasped, but soon they were repeating what he had said. "The Emperor has nothing on!" they whispered, until at last the whole crowd cried out, "The Emperor has lost his clothes!"

The Emperor turned a deep shade of pink all over, for he knew it was the truth. But he was far too proud to admit his foolish vanity, so he just stuck his nose in the air and marched home, with this chamberlains still carrying his invisible train behind him!

I Love Little Pussy

I love little pussy, her coat is so warm,
And if I don't hurt her she'll do me no harm,
So I'll not pull her tail nor drive her away,
But pussy and I very gently will play.

Tom Thumb

Once upon a time there lived a poor woodman and his wife. They were very sad, for they longed to have children of their own.

"How lonely it is!" said the woodman's wife. "I should be happy, even if we had a child who was no bigger than my thumb!"

One day this woman's wish came true, for not long after she had a little boy who was strong and healthy, but no bigger than her thumb.

"I shall call him Tom Thumb," she said.

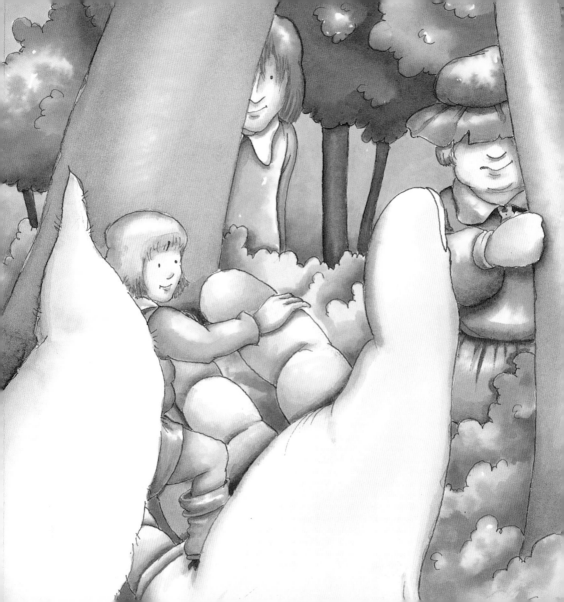

One day Tom was in the forest with his father when two men saw him. They wanted to buy Tom and offered his father a big bag of gold for him, but his father was not happy.

"Take the money," said Tom. "I will soon find a way to come back to you."

So the men took Tom with them, but after a while they let him down to stretch his legs. Quick as a flash, Tom ran into a mouse hole and hid until the men had gone.

That night he slept in an empty snail shell that he found nearby.

Later that night Tom was woken by some robbers who were planning to steal all the gold from the parson's house.

"Hey there!" called Tom. "I can help you!"

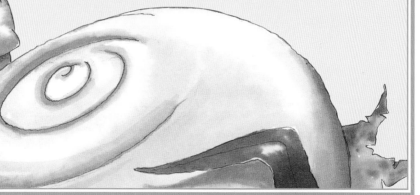

The robbers took Tom to the parson's house, and he crawled through the bars on the window.

"Do you want all the gold?" Tom yelled. He shouted so loudly that he woke the cook, and the robbers ran off as fast as they could. Tom laughed and laughed. That night he went to sleep in a nice, warm barn.

The next morning Tom woke up and found himself inside a cow's stomach. The cow had not seen him asleep in the hay she was eating.

"Let me out!" he shouted, scaring the poor milkmaid so much that she fell off her stool! Everyone thought the poor cow had gone mad and so it was killed. The cow's stomach was thrown on a rubbish heap where it was eaten by a wolf, so Tom was no better off, but he soon made a plan to escape.

"Hey, Mr Wolf," called Tom. "Are you still hungry?"

The wolf said he was very hungry so Tom directed him to his own house where there was always a lot to eat. That night the wolf crept into the kitchen and helped himself to all the goodies that he found there. But he ate so much that he couldn't fit through the door to get out again!

Tom laughed so loudly that his parents woke up and came running down the stairs.

In no time Tom's father had killed the wicked old wolf with an axe. They cut open his stomach and out jumped their very own Tom Thumb! How pleased they were to see each other again! "Adventures are all very well," said Tom happily. "But there is no place like home!"

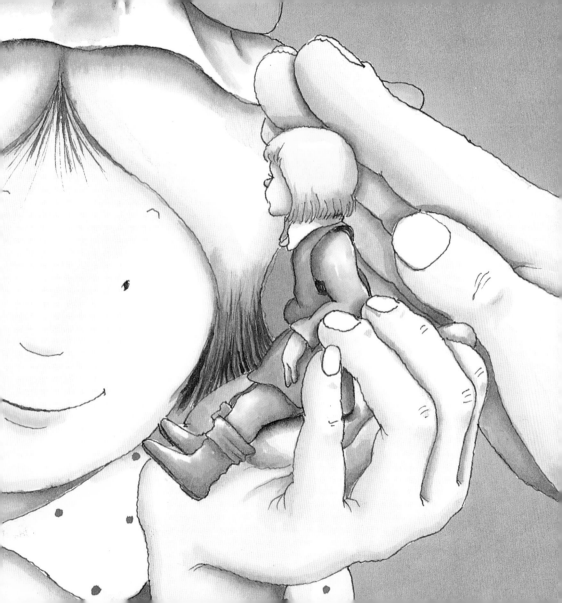

Pussy Cat, Pussy Cat

Pussy cat, pussy cat, where have you been?
I've been up to London to visit the Queen.
Pussy cat, pussy cat, what did you there?
I frightened a little mouse under her chair.

DESMOND THE DRAGON

Young Desmond the Dragon was by now almost nearly sure that he wasn't a dragon. He was covered with tough, green scales. He had a forked tongue, just like all his friends, and fine claws, as well as a good loud dragon-type roar. But, despite all this, Desmond was still worried that he might not be a real dragon.

Each morning he looked in the mirror, twisting around to examine his back and each morning he saw – nothing. Dragons had wings, didn't they? If he was a dragon, where were his wings? Then Desmond would go outside the cave into the garden and breathe out hard. Nothing. Dragons breathed fire, didn't they? If he was a dragon, where was his fire? Poor Desmond was very confused.

Then one day Desmond woke up with a fang-ache. He looked in the mirror and saw a huge swelling on the side of his face. Desmond rushed downstairs to his mum.

"Mum," he mumbled, "look at my face. It has gone all lumpy and bumpy."

Desmond's mum looked at his face and said, "Oh dear, I think you have been eating too many chocolate-covered bones. We'd better go and see Morris the Magician. He's a wonderful fangtist, amongst other things."

She winked at Desmond's dad, and while Desmond went to get his hat, said to him, "I think it's time to get a couple of other things sorted out too while we're there, don't you, dear?"

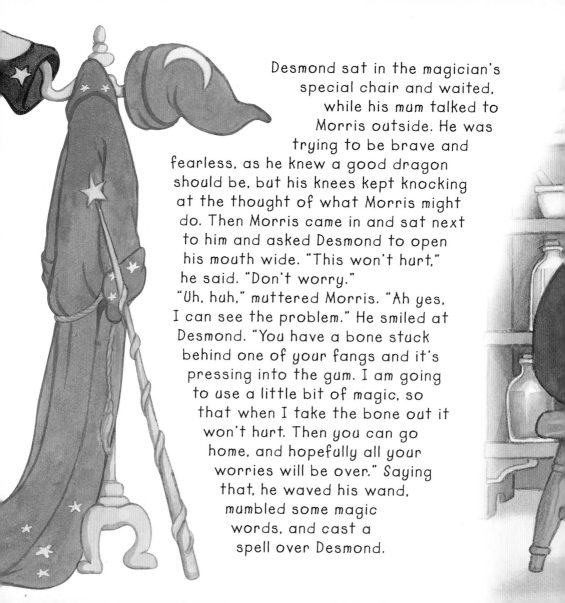

Desmond sat in the magician's special chair and waited, while his mum talked to Morris outside. He was trying to be brave and fearless, as he knew a good dragon should be, but his knees kept knocking at the thought of what Morris might do. Then Morris came in and sat next to him and asked Desmond to open his mouth wide. "This won't hurt," he said. "Don't worry."

"Uh, huh," muttered Morris. "Ah yes, I can see the problem." He smiled at Desmond. "You have a bone stuck behind one of your fangs and it's pressing into the gum. I am going to use a little bit of magic, so that when I take the bone out it won't hurt. Then you can go home, and hopefully all your worries will be over." Saying that, he waved his wand, mumbled some magic words, and cast a spell over Desmond.

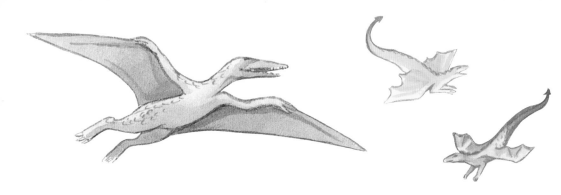

Some time later, Desmond opened his eyes. Looking around, he slowly remembered where he was. Pleased to discover the bone gone he breathed a great sigh of relief, and a huge ball of flames came shooting out! Fortunately, he didn't burn anything.

"Look, look," he shouted. "See, I am a dragon. I can breathe fire!" and he beamed at his mum and Morris.

Morris smiled a secret magician's smile and exchanged a knowing look with Mrs Dragon. "Of course you can," he said. "We always knew you would when the time was right. You can't hurry these things you know. I think you will find that you can unfold your wings now as well."

Desmond looked at Morris mystified.

Mrs Dragon thanked the magician and she and Desmond went outside. Then, without thinking, Desmond unfurled his tightly folded wings – they had been there all along. He nearly fell over with surprise. Desmond's mum smiled. "I think you're ready to try flying now. Perhaps we can practice on the way home."

Excitedly, Desmond waved goodbye to Morris, who,
still smiling a secret magician's smile, was watching from
his window.
Desmond opened his wings and wobbled into the air.
Then, his confidence growing, he soared up into the sky
and flew round a few times – looking and feeling like the
noble dragon he was.
And finally, he flew home for tea with his mum and dad.

Six Little Mice

Six little mice sat down to spin,
Pussy passed by, and she peeped in.
"What are you at, my little men?"
"Making coats for gentlemen."
"Shall I come in and bite off your threads?"
"No, no Miss Pussy you'll snip off our heads!"
"Oh, no, I'll not, I'll help you to spin."
"That may be so, but you don't come in!"

The Steadfast Tin Soldier

There was once a Tin Soldier. He was exactly the same as his twenty-four brothers, but for one thing. He had only one leg! When he was made, the tin ran out just as it was about to be poured into his second leg, but he could still stand straight and tall.

He lived in the nursery with all the other toys, but his favourite was a pretty little Dancer made of paper. She stood on one toe and pointed her other foot high in the air, almost as if she had only one leg, just like him! The Steadfast Tin Soldier loved to watch her and stood perfectly still for hour after hour gazing at her lovely face and wishing he could find the courage to speak to her.

The toys belonged to a little boy. At night when he was fast asleep the toys came to life and filled the room with spinning tops, bouncing balls and dancing dolls. But there were two toys who did not move – the Tin Soldier and the pretty Dancer. They stood quiet and still, each on their one leg, as they gazed silently at each other. Suddenly the clock chimed midnight and a little black imp appeared. s very rude to stare at the Dancer like that," he told the Tin Soldier.

But the Tin Soldier ignored him and carried on staring. The Imp stamped his foot angrily. "You just wait. You will learn your lesson tomorrow!" said the Imp.

The next day the little boy played with the Tin Soldier and when he went for his tea he left him standing by the window. Now whether it was the wind or whether it was the little black imp up to his tricks, who can say, but all of a sudden the window flew open and the Soldier was blown outside! Down he tumbled and landed with a bump upside down between two paving stones. There he stayed, firmly wedged, and soon it began to rain.

When the rain stopped two little boys found him, and made a paper boat for him to sail in, and he whooshed along the gutter.
All of a sudden the boat entered a dark tunnel and the boys' excited shouts were left far behind.

The Tin Soldier felt very frightened, but he stood up straight and tall. Suddenly a great water rat appeared and the Tin Soldier thought his end had come. But the boat sped on out into the light once more and over a great waterfall, for this was where the gutter emptied into the canal. The paper boat fell apart and the Tin Soldier sank below the water, still standing proudly to attention, and thinking only of the little Dancer. Suddenly the Tin Soldier heard a loud gulp! He had been swallowed by a fish! The fish began to twist this way and that and then all was still once again.

The hours passed and just when the Tin Soldier thought he was lost forever there was a flash of light and he found himself lying on a table. The fish had been caught and taken to market. And now it was lying on a kitchen table, ready to be prepared and cooked.

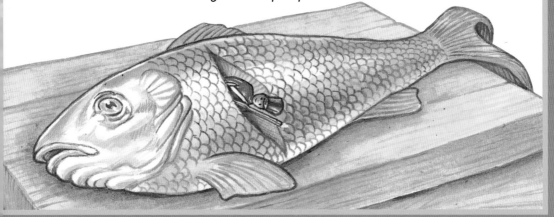

"It's a little Tin Soldier," exclaimed the cook. "I will take him up to the nursery." To his amazement, the Tin Soldier found himself back in his old nursery and there was the pretty Dancer still standing on one toe.

But the little boy was not pleased to see him. Maybe it was because he looked so shabby, or maybe the little black imp had something to do with it, but he snatched up the Tin Soldier and threw him in the fire!
There he stood tall and brave as the flames flickered around him. He looked straight at the Dancer and she looked right back at him. Suddenly the door opened and a draught blew the paper Dancer into the fire where she landed in the arms of the Tin Soldier.

In the grate the next morning the little boy found a whisp of black paper and a small lump of tin in the shape of a heart – all that was left of the Dancer and her Steadfast Tin Soldier

Baa Baa Black Sheep

Baa baa black sheep
Have you any wool?
Yes, sir, yes, sir, three bags full;
One for the master and one for the dame,
And one for the little boy
Who lives down the lane.

There Was A Crooked Man

There was a crooked man,
And he walked a crooked mile,
He found a crooked sixpence
Against a crooked stile.
He brought a crooked cat,
Which caught a crooked mouse,
And they all lived together
In a little crooked house.

Bulky the Giant ★

Bulky was a gentle giant. He was always polite
to the local villagers and did his best not to
upset them, which, being huge, wasn't easy.
Take Bulky's feet, for instance. His shoes
seemed like boats to the villagers. Even if
Bulky tiptoed past their homes, he still
made the ground tremble. The startled
folk fell out of bed, kitchen
crockery rattled and furniture
bounced about.

The villagers complained to Bulky.
They only dared to because he was
so nice and kind. He even said sorry
and promised to creep around more
carefully than before.

"I should think so," said the villagers,
impatiently.

Then there was his sneezing. When Bulky sneezed he
sent such a blast of air howling across the valley,
the villagers had to rush indoors for fear of being
blown away!
The giant had promised he would sneeze into his hanky,
but sometimes a sneeze came upon him all of a sudden,
before he could do anything about it.
Eventually the villagers decided life would be more
comfortable without a giant living on their doorstep.

So Bulky agreed to let Spellbound the Wizard shrink him, and with a wave of Spellbound's wand he shrank to the same size as the delighted villagers! For a while everyone lived peacefully.

Bulky moved in with a kind family who looked after him very well, and he began to enjoy life at his new size.

But a nasty big surprise was in store for them when a new giant appeared from beyond the mountains. Heavyhand was bad-tempered and mean. He stomped about, flattening crops, and knocking down trees. The stink of his smelly feet wafted through the valley, sending everyone indoors. And when he slept, he snored louder than thunder. The villagers tried to complain, but Heavyhand roared angrily at them and warned that if he wasn't left in peace, he would flatten every home in the village!

"I like this valley," he bellowed. "And I'm here to stay!"
The villagers huddled in their homes, trembling with fear.
"If only Bulky were still big, he'd soon see off
Heavyhand!" they whispered.
But Spellbound said it would take some time to reverse
the spell.
"We can't wait," replied Bulky, "Heavyhand is causing too
much trouble. I've an idea! Listen carefully..."

As Heavyhand lay snoring he felt something tickle his nose. Snuffling and snorting, he opened his eyes and saw a little figure laughing at him and waving a feather. It was Bulky. "I tickled you!" he called cheekily. "Can't catch me!"

He leapt onto a horse he'd left nearby, and raced for the mountains, while a furious Heavyhand reached for his boots. By the time he caught up, Bulky was heading into a huge cave, and Heavyhand followed in hot pursuit. But Bulky knew another way out, if you were small enough. As Bulky scrambled out free, the villagers pushed against a rock high above the cave, starting an avalanche falling in front of the cave mouth.

"Heavyhand is trapped!" cried the villagers. But not for long!

The mountain trembled as Heavyhand raged and cursed,
and began to dig himself out. He worked all day and
night. So did Spellbound, until at last his spell was ready.
With a wave of his wand Bulky began to grow, just as
Heavyhand came bursting from the cave. Imagine his
surprise when he saw Bulky standing a good head and
shoulders above him. Even for a giant, Bulky was big.
"Go and find your own valley. This one's mine!" roared
Bulky. Heavyhand didn't stop to argue, but took off
nervously across the mountains without looking back.
   "We promise never to complain again, Bulky," the
thankful villagers told him. "We know we made a big
mistake before!"
   "More like a giant one!" someone joked and everyone
laughed, though Bulky took care not to laugh too loudly.

There Was An Old Woman...

There was an old woman who lived in a shoe,
She had so many children
she didn't know what to do;
She gave them some broth without any bread,
And kissed them all soundly
And put them to bed.

Hansel and Grettel

Once upon a time there was a poor woodcutter who
lived in the woods with his two children, and their
horrible stepmother. The woodcutter had very little
money for food and so all four of them went hungry
for much of the time.

Late one night as the two children lay shivering in their
beds they heard their stepmother make a terrible
suggestion. They could no longer afford to feed their
children so they would take them deep into the
woods and leave them there so that they
would not be able to find their way
home. After arguing for many hours
their poor father finally agreed
to her plan.

Grettel wept bitterly and her
brother Hansel comforted
her. "I will find a way
home, little sister,"
he said, and he
made a plan.

The next morning the children were taken far away into the woods.

"Stay here until we return," said their stepmother. Soon night fell and they were left alone. Poor Grettel sobbed as if her heart would break.

"Dry your eyes," said Hansel. "On the way here I dropped a white pebble on the ground every few steps. See how they shine in the moonlight. We can follow the trail home." Soon they arrived back home.

Their father was overjoyed to see them
for he was ashamed of leaving them,
and their stepmother pretended to
be pleased also.
But that night they overheard
their parents arguing again.
"The children must be got
rid of or we'll all starve,"
said their stepmother.
"We'll take them deeper
into the wood
tomorrow."
Sadly their father
was forced to
give in.

This time Hansel did not have time to collect any white pebbles, so when they were led into the forest he dropped a trail of crumbled bread for them to follow that night. But later when they searched for the crumbs they were alarmed to find them gone, for the birds had eaten every one! Try as they might the frightened children could not find their way home. Again and again they tried to find a way out of the forest but every path they took led them ever deeper into the wood. Just then Hansel saw a white dove on a branch. The bird sang so sweetly that the children stopped and listened, then followed her as she flew on deep into the heart of the wood, until they came to a little gingerbread cottage. Its roof was made of honey cake and the windows were all of barley sugar!

Soon they were munching away on parts of the house and nothing had ever tasted so delicious.

Suddenly the door flew open and an old woman hobbled out. Hansel and Grettel were terrified but the old lady smiled and invited them inside. She fed them sweet pancakes, then put them to bed under cosy quilts. But when they awoke next day the old lady's kind manner had changed. Her eyes gleamed as she grabbed Hansel's arm. "You will make a tasty morsel for me to eat," she cackled and then the children saw that they had been tricked. The old lady was a witch and she meant to make a meal of them! Laughing cruelly, she bundled Hansel into a cage. "I will fatten you up before I cook you," she hissed and Hansel shook with fear. Every day she told him to hold his finger out, so she could feel how fat he was getting. But her eyesight was terrible and she could not see that he always held out a bone for her to feel. She could not understand how he stayed so thin.

At last the witch could wait no longer.
"Fat or thin, I will eat him as he is," she decided. Poor
Grettel cried and cried, but the witch took no notice.
Pushing Grettel toward the oven, the wicked witch
told her to creep inside and see if it was
hot enough. But Grettel guessed she
was also on the menu and thinking
quickly, asked the witch how
to get inside.
"Silly goose," said the witch,
poking her head into the
oven, "I could easily get in
myself." Grettel gave her a
great shove, and pushed the
witch right inside the oven.
She slammed the door
tight shut, and that was
the end of the wicked
old witch!
Grettel ran straight
to Hansel's cage and
opened the door.
How they rejoiced to
be free once again!

Then the two children explored the cottage, and found chests full of treasure in every corner! They stuffed their pockets to the brim with jewels and Grettel filled her apron.

Soon they were ready and they set off to find their way home. They wandered for hours until at last the wood became more familiar to them. A kind white duck carried them across the river. Then in the distance they saw their father's house, and began to run. Their father was overjoyed to see them. He had not had a single happy hour since he had left them, and in that time their selfish stepmother had died. They emptied out their pockets and precious jewels rolled all over the floor. Their father hugged them and they all laughed for joy.

And so their troubles were ended and they all lived happily ever after.

Old King Cole

Old King Cole was a merry old soul,
And a merry old soul was he;
He called for his pipe,
And he called for his bowl,
And he called for his fiddlers three.

Sing a Song of Sixpence

Sing a song of sixpence,
A pocket full of rye;
Four-and-twenty blackbirds baked in a pie;
When the pie was opened,
The birds began to sing;
Was not that a dainty dish,
To set before a king?

Magic Mix Up ★

Wanda the Witch climbed out of bed and put on her shabby old black dress. She tied a belt round her plump belly and pushed her hair up into her pointy hat – it was too tangled to brush it. "What a mess," she said. "Still, I've no time to waste on myself." Wanda was always busy doing spells for her friends. But her wand had never been quite the same since it fell into her cauldron and her spells often got in a muddle.

This morning she had a birthday cake spell to do for young Harry Hedgehog's party. She peered at the recipe in her spellbook. "Large frog, cup of rats' tails, slimy slugs, and a pretty flower. Mix together, throw mixture into the air, wave your wand and say the magic words. Sounds simple. I just need to go and pick a flower."

Wanda headed into the forest and soon found some flowers to pick. Then she heard someone humming. Peeping out from behind a tree, she saw the beautiful Princess Primula, who had long golden hair, big brown eyes, dainty little hands and a gorgeous sparkly pink gown. But when Princess Primula saw Wanda watching her she screamed and ran away as fast as she could. "I must have scared her. She is so beautiful and I'm so ugly."
A tear rolled down Wanda's cheek. Then she had an idea.

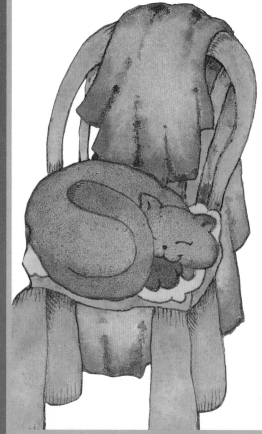

"I'm always doing magic
for other people.
I should do some for
myself. I'll go home and
find a spell to make
myself as beautiful as
the princess."

Back at home, she soon found a spell to make lovely long hair. She took off her hat, picked up her wand and said the magic words. But when she felt her head, instead of soft silky hair, she felt something smooth and shiny. She was completely bald!

"Oh bother," she cried. "This stupid wand. I'll have to buy a new one! Oh well, I'll come back to my hair later. I think I'll try making my hands and feet smaller."

She said the magic words, but when she held out her arms there at the end were two dainty little feet. When she stuck out her legs there were two pretty hands on the end of each.

"Drat and blast. What a muddle. I'll try a spell to make me thinner."

With a wave of her wand she was instantly so thin that her dress fell off her shoulders and onto the floor. Wanda was left standing in the kitchen in just her underwear!

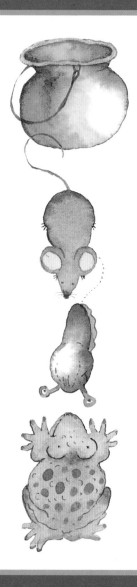

At that moment Harriet Hedgehog arrived to fetch her son's cake. She took one look at Wanda and burst out laughing. "What on earth are you doing?"

"I was trying to make myself beautiful," replied Wanda, and she explained what had happened in the forest.

"Well, Princess Primula may be beautiful on the outside, but she's horrible inside. She's mean and selfish and nobody likes her," said Harriet. "You may not be beautiful but you are kind and helpful and everybody loves you."

Wanda thought about this. "You're right. I do have a lot of friends, and that's what matters most. I'd better get out of this muddle and get on with Harry's cake."

Wanda cancelled all the spells, and in no time had conjured up a big, gooey cake.

"At last a spell that's worked! Now I'd better hurry and get ready for the party."

Wanda made an
effort to look
the best she could,
but without using any
magic this time! She put on
a sparkly new dress with gold moons, and
a pair of purple boots.
She looked in the mirror and smiled.
"I'm not so ugly after all," she said to herself. "But I
realise now that being beautiful inside is
more important."
At the party everyone tucked into the
cake and told her how lovely she looked.
Then Harry handed Wanda a parcel.
"But it's not my birthday," she said.
"It's to show you we love you," said Harry.
It was a wonderful new wand. "You
won't get your spells muddled now,"
laughed Harriet. Wanda thanked them
all and felt very lucky to have so
many friends. She spent the
afternoon doing spells with her
new wand, entertaining everyone at
the party, and of course, eating
lots of cake!

Three Young Rats

Three young rats with black felt hats,
Three young ducks with white straw flats;
Three young dogs with curling tails,
Three young cats with demi-veils;
Went out to walk with two young pigs
In satin vests and sorrel wigs,
But suddenly it chanced to rain
And so they all went home again.

Rumpelstiltskin

Once there was a poor miller who had a beautiful daughter. One day the King came riding by, and to impress him the miller foolishly boasted that his daughter could spin straw into gold! Now, the King loved gold, and was very greedy, so he ordered the miller to bring the girl to his palace where he would put her to the test.

The King led the girl into a room filled with a huge mound of straw and an old spinning-wheel. "Spin this straw into gold before morning," he said. "Or you will die," and he locked the door behind her.

The poor girl had no idea what to do, so she put her head in her hands and cried.

Suddenly the door opened and in walked a tiny little man. He offered to help in return for a gift, so she gave him her necklace, and in no time at all he spun the straw into gold.

Next morning, the King was delighted. He ordered the poor girl to stay another night and locked her in a larger room with an even bigger pile of straw. The little man appeared again, and this time he spun the straw into gold in exchange for her gold ring. The greedy King was so excited that the next night he locked her in an even larger room with an even bigger pile of straw. "Spin this into gold before morning and you shall be my Queen!" he said.

For a third time the girl wept until the little man appeared again, but this time she had nothing left to give him. So the little man offered to work in exchange for a promise.

"Promise that if you become Queen you will give me your first-born child," he said. The girl felt she had no other choice, so she agreed and the little man set to work.

"Besides, I may never become Queen, or have children," she thought to herself.

Next morning the King was overjoyed to see so much treasure and he made the girl his wife that very day. The King and Queen lived happily with their great riches and soon the miller's daughter had forgotten all about her promise. Then, one year later, the Queen gave birth to a beautiful baby daughter and she was filled with happiness. But as she sat gently singing to the baby, the door suddenly blew open and in marched the little man.

"I have come to remind you of your promise," he declared. Then the poor Queen remembered the bargain that she had struck long ago in the room full of straw.

"You may have anything else you wish!" she cried.

"Treasure, jewels, gold – just ask and it shall be yours!" But the little man remained firm, and would take nothing else.

Then the Queen sobbed so hard that her tears softened the little man's heart.

"You have three days to discover my name," he said. "Or I will claim your daughter."

So the Queen summoned her messengers, and sent them out to discover the strangest names they could find. When the the little man arrived next day, she asked:

"Is your name Ichabod or Jeremiah? Maybe Caspar, Melchior or Balthazar?"

"That is not my name," he replied. "You have two more days to discover it."

So the Queen sent her messengers out once more, and next day had a new list for him. "Are you called Noddy, Sheepshanks, or Old Bandylegs?" she asked. "How about Hunchback or Crookshanks or Shortribs?"

But the little man just shook his head. "That is not my name," he replied. "You have one more day to find it out."

That evening the Queen sat pale and tired as her messengers read out long lists of names. Then a young messenger burst in, trembling with excitement, and told the Queen he had seen a little man dancing around a fire deep in the woods and singing:

'Merrily the feast I'll make,
Today I'll brew, tomorrow bake.
Merrily I'll dance and sing,
For next day will a stranger bring
The Queen's own child, so fair and sweet,
And then my joy will be complete.
Little does my Lady dream
That Rumpelstiltskin is my name!'

The Queen jumped for joy. At last she had discovered the little man's name!

Next day she teased the little man, "Is your name John? Or Tom? Or Jemmy?"

"It is not," replied the little man.

"Then perhaps it is – Rumpelstiltskin!" cried the Queen. The little man gnashed his teeth with rage and stomped and screamed. He stamped his feet so hard that the floor gave way beneath him, and he disappeared through it. And that was the end of Rumpelstiltskin!

The Queen of Hearts

The Queen of Hearts,
She made some tarts,
All on a summer's day;
The Knave of Hearts,
He stole those tarts,
And took them clean away.

ONE DRAGON TOO MANY

There once was a land which was ruled by an old
king. It had mountains and forests, a castle, and just
the right amount of strange creatures to make it a
proper fairytale kingdom. This made the old king very
happy, as he took great pride in his work.

Once a month, he took out his Great Big Account
Book and ticked off the things in his kingdom.
A wishing well (tick!), a unicorn (tick!), five fairies
(tick!), a wicked witch (tick!), a fierce lion
(tick!), a family of giants (tick!), two dragons
(tick! and tick!), and a young prince/heir to
the throne/son type thing (...er...tick!).

But one day when he got to "two
dragons" (tick!), he noticed that it
now read, "three dragons." He
didn't, of course, tick that.

Three dragons was far too
many for a small fairytale
kingdom. It said so in his
How to Rule a Proper
Fairytale Kingdom manual.

So the old king sent for his son.

"I want you to seek out a dragon and kill it," said the old king. "We've got too many."

"Are you sure?" asked the young prince, a bit taken aback.

"Quite sure!" said the old king. "And it says here in my manual that young princes are supposed to seek out and dispose of any excess dragons. It's part of their job."

So off went the young prince. He wasn't too happy about it. He'd never killed anything in his young and princely life, and he wasn't really sure he wanted to.

But he put on his silver armour, climbed on his horse, and off he went. He looked terrific, just like a young prince should.

After a long journey, the
young prince arrived at the
place on his map marked 'Here Be
Dragons.' He got down from his horse
and walked towards a cave.
"Hello? Dragons? Are you home?" he called
into the cave.
"Hold on," said a voice. "I'll be right out."
After a moment, a dragon came out of the
cave. It wasn't a very big dragon at all,
and the young prince was quite
disappointed (and rather pleased at the
same time).
Still, it was a real dragon, with a mouthful
of fangs, a coat of shiny green scales, and
a pair of tiny wings. When it spoke, little
flames crackled along its forked tongue.
The young prince and the small dragon
introduced themselves and shook hands.
Soon they were sitting sipping
lemonade and talking like old friends.

"So what can I do for you, Young Prince?" asked the small dragon.

"I'm afraid my mum and dad, the big dragons, are out at the moment. Princesses to menace, villages to burn with their flaming breath ... you know how it is."

"Well, you see, the thing is ..." began the young prince. "Actually, I've got to find a dragon and kill it. Dad says I must."

"Oh!" said the small dragon.

"Sorry," said the young prince.

"I wouldn't want you to disobey your dad, of course, but is there any way we could skip the actual 'killing a dragon' bit?" asked the small dragon.

"I don't know," said the young prince, thoughtfully. "It depends. Can you play hide and seek?"

When the young prince got home, the old king
had the Great Big Account Book open ready.
"Dragons?" he asked, sternly.
"Two," said the young prince.
"Tick! Well done!" said the old king.
"You'd better add a new bit to your accounts,
though," said the young prince. "Friends of
the young prince/heir to the throne/son
type of thing."
"How many?" asked the old king.
"One," said the prince, smiling.
"Made a friend, did you?" asked the
old king, closing the Great Big
Account Book and looking up
with a smile.
"Yes," said the young prince.
"One who's much better at
hiding than I am at seeking."
And from that day on, there
have been the right number
of ticks in the old
king's book.

This Little Pig

This little pig went to market;
This little pig stayed at home;
This little pig had roast beef;
This little pig had none;
And this little pig cried,
"Wee, wee, wee!" All the way home.

Mary Had a Little Lamb

Mary had a little lamb
With fleece as white as snow,
And everywhere that Mary went,
The lamb was sure to go.

The Sorcerer's Apprentice

Once there was a man who had so much work that he was busy from sunrise to sunset. So he went to town to find an apprentice to help in his workshop.

"Can you read and write?" the man asked a young boy, who was looking for work.

"Why, yes!" replied the boy, who was called Hans.

"What a pity!" sighed the man. "I don't want an apprentice who can read and write." Hans thought quickly. "I can't read or write. I thought you said eat and fight!"

"Excellent!" cried the man. "Then you are just the boy for me."

They set off into the forest, and walked until they reached a dark castle. Now, Hans had only pretended not to read and write, and was curious to find out why the man wanted an ignorant helper.

But when the man led him into his workshop, it soon became clear! Inside there was a huge black cauldron hanging over a fire. Bookshelves were filled with dusty books, jars of strange objects covered the floor, and in the corner was a tall pointed hat! The man was a sorcerer, and Hans guessed he did not want an apprentice who could read his spells! So he pretended to be stupid, while trying to learn all he could.

Hans did many jobs for his master. He stirred the foul mixtures bubbling in the cauldron. He ground up herbs – and other nasty things! He swept the workshop, tended the fire and gathered strange ingredients for the magician's potions. But the job he hated most of all was filling the huge cauldron with water. It was so wide and deep that it needed bucket after bucket and each one had to be fetched from a well deep in the deepest dungeon of the castle.

Hans longed to look at the magic books, but he didn't dare as he had told the magician that he could not read or write. Then one day the sorcerer went out, saying he would return that night. "Take good care of my workshop!" he ordered.

As soon as he was gone, Hans took down a big spellbook and had soon found an interesting spell – "How to find an Extra Pair of Hands." Hans looked at the empty cauldron that was waiting to be filled with water. If only he had an extra pair of hands he could do the job in no time. Following the spell, he fetched a broom, and said the magic words. Suddenly it grew two arms from its handle and stood up straight on its bristles. With a cry of delight Hans handed it two buckets. "Fetch me water from the well and fill the empty cauldron!" he commanded and instantly the broom marched out of the room and down the steps to the dungeon.

Soon Hans could hear it climbing back up the steps and it appeared with two full buckets which it tipped into the huge cauldron. He clapped his hands with glee. The broom made trip after trip and soon the cauldron was full to the brim.

"That's enough!" said Hans, but the broom kept on going. "No more! Stop!" cried Hans, but the broom had been told to fetch water and that is what it was doing! Soon the cauldron was overflowing and had spilled all over the floor.

Hans searched frantically through the spellbook for the magic word to stop the spell, but he could not find a clue. So he grabbed an axe and chopped the broom in two. But to his alarm, each half grew arms and buckets and set off back down the steps. He raced after them and smashed the wood into tiny splinters. But each splinter grew, and formed arms and buckets and soon a whole army was marching down the steps.

Hans ran around in a panic. He tried to block the door but the marching brooms were too strong and pushed him aside. Soon the whole workshop was awash. The poor sorcerer's apprentice put his head in his hands and wept as the water swirled around him. Then suddenly he heard the castle door creak open. The sorcerer had returned! His eyes shone angrily as he entered his watery workshop, and poor Hans shook in his boots. The sorcerer waved his wand, uttered some magic words, and in a flash the brooms disappeared. The water swirled out of the workshop and back into the well. Ashamed, Hans bowed his head as he explained what had happened. But to his great surprise, the sorcerer laughed. "I was young once," he said, "and I was just as curious as you. I will teach you to become a great sorcerer like me on one condition – no more spells until you are ready!" and this time Hans quite happily agreed!

Little Boy Blue

Little Boy Blue, come blow your horn
The sheep's in the meadow, the cow's in the corn.
Where is the boy who looks after the sheep?
He's under the haystack fast asleep.
Will you wake him? No, not I!
For if I do, he's sure to cry.

JACK AND THE BEANSTALK

Once upon a time there lived a poor widow and her lazy son Jack. He would not work, and so there came a time when they had no money left for food.

"All we have left to sell is our cow," said Jack's mother, and so the next day Jack took the cow to market, where he sold her for a handful of beans. He took the beans home to his mother, but she was so angry that she threw them out of the window.

"We cannot live on a handful of beans!" she cried, and they went to bed that night very hungry indeed. But when Jack woke next morning all he could see from his window were huge green leaves. The beans had grown into a giant beanstalk, which reached high into the sky.

"I am going to climb up and see where it ends," decided Jack, and began to climb.

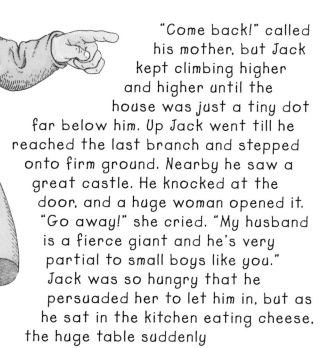

"Come back!" called his mother, but Jack kept climbing higher and higher until the house was just a tiny dot far below him. Up Jack went till he reached the last branch and stepped onto firm ground. Nearby he saw a great castle. He knocked at the door, and a huge woman opened it. "Go away!" she cried. "My husband is a fierce giant and he's very partial to small boys like you." Jack was so hungry that he persuaded her to let him in, but as he sat in the kitchen eating cheese, the huge table suddenly shook and a loud roar filled the air. "Fee, fi, fo, fum, I smell the blood of an Englishman! Be he alive or be dead, I'll grind his bones to make my bread!" "Hurry up and hide!" whispered the terrified woman. "My husband is coming!" She bundled Jack into the oven as an enormous giant strode into the kitchen.

"It's just the smell of your breakfast, dear!" said his wife anxiously. Jack sat silently trembling as the giant gobbled his breakfast, then told his wife to fetch his hen.

"Lay!" ordered the giant and to Jack's astonishment the hen laid an egg at once. But this was no ordinary egg – it was a golden egg! The giant smiled greedily. Then he yawned loudly, laid his great head upon his arms, and was soon fast asleep. Jack leapt out of the oven and grabbed the hen, then he raced from the kitchen and out of the huge castle door.

He ran for the beanstalk as fast as his legs could carry him and in no time at all he was back home with the hen still tucked tightly beneath his arm. "Look, mother!" he cried. "This hen will lay as many golden eggs as we wish. We need never go hungry again."

After a time Jack grew eager for adventure, so disguising himself, he climbed the beanstalk, and persuaded the giant's foolish wife to let him in once more. But as he sat at the kitchen table, he heard a roar:

"Fee, fi, fo fum, I smell the blood of an Englishman!" The giant was coming! Quickly Jack ran and hid in the oven. He peeked out as the giant gulped down his meal.

"Bring me my money bags!" cried the giant.

Slowly he counted piles of glittering golden coins but then he began to yawn and soon he was fast asleep. Jack jumped out of his hiding place, heaved a large money bag over his shoulder and ran like the wind away from the castle.

His mother was very thankful to see him safe and sound and what fun they had that night as they counted their new riches over and over again.

But after a time Jack grew restless, so disguising himself again, he climbed the beanstalk once more. The giant's wife was wary, as she had been tricked twice already, but Jack soon charmed her and she let him in again. This time he tried to steal the giant's golden harp, which played the sweetest music Jack had ever heard. But as he ran from the room, the harp called out,

"Master! Master!" With a cry of rage the giant awoke and stumbled after Jack. Out of the castle and down the beanstalk the terrified boy ran, with the giant close behind him.

"Quick, mother, fetch the axe!" Jack shouted as he neared the ground. He swung the axe high in the air and with one mighty blow felled the plant. The giant gave a loud cry, then tumbled from its branches and landed headfirst on the ground, stone dead. And from that time on Jack and his mother lived happily ever after.

Wee Willie Winkie

Wee Willie Winkie runs through the town,
Upstairs and downstairs in his nightgown,
Rapping at the windows, crying through the locks,
"Are the children in their beds,
It's past eight o'clock?"

Twinkle, Twinkle, Little Star

Twinkle, twinkle, little star
How I wonder what you are!
Up above the moon so high
Like a diamond in the sky.

The End

This book was written by:
Charles Perrault; Amber Hunt; Candy Wallace; Brothers Grimm;
Hans Christian Andersen; Dan Abnett; Geoff Cowan; Claire Steeden
Aladdin and the Magic Lamp & Ali Baba and the Forty Thieves both from
The Tales of the Arabian Nights.

This book was illustrated by:
Rhymes: Angela Kincaid. Stories: Caroline Sharpe; Claire Mumford;
Helen Cockburn; Diana Catchpole; Annabel Spenceley; Jenny Press; Roger Langton;
Rodney Shaw; Nigel McMullen; Helen Smith; Douglas Cameron; Dave Anstey.